My Weird School Special

There's a Skunk in My Bunk!

Dan Gutman

Pictures by
Jim Paillot

HARPER

An Imprint of HarperCollinsPublishers

To Hudson Brotspies, Andi Kristall, Dan McKenzie, Lee Rozenbaunn, and Derek Scarcella

Thanks to Yvonne Mary Albright, Sarah Lewandowski-Barthel, Julie Beck, Mandy Carter Chase, Elizabeth Compton, Dave Darde, Kate Did, Janet Chaille Dietz, Jennifer Dorfberger, Reb Ecca, Jessica Edwards, Heather Fischer, Kerry Furney, Eliana Knazan Garry, Susan Ghali, Brittany Gillen, Kathleen Guinnane, Tracy Hengst, Anne Higgins, Rachel Hurley, Gwen Jones, Michele Shelly Kierman-Karver, Sarah Keesler, Christine Kirk, Amanda Leatherman, Kathleen Hanrahan Lorenzo, Joslyn Sheridan Mathison, Jillian Hutchens Mors, Anne Murray, Kimberly Nguyen, Patricia Ohanian, Jeena Kunjappu Pereira, Jean Peretzman, Jacquelynn Pleis, Erin Moss Plouzek, Hen Rasmussen, Janine Gaudette Roode, Peggy McAndrew Rush, Beth Schultz, Laura Schwartzkopf, Shannon Glass Searle, Anne Seikel, Tara Weiss Senker, Kirsten Budke Shivak, Geiza Ferreira Shulkin, Randy Steinman, Sharon Foy Swanke, Michelle Dowd Torosian, Patti Parnell Young, Erica Petersen Yuengling.

My Weird School Special: There's a Skunk in My Bunk!
Text copyright © 2024 by Dan Gutman
Illustrations copyright © 2024 by Jim Paillot
All rights reserved. Printed in the United States of America.
No part of this book may be used or reproduced in any manner whatsoever without written permission except in the case of brief quotations embodied in critical articles and reviews. For information address HarperCollins Children's Books, a division of HarperCollins Publishers, 195 Broadway, New York, NY 10007.
www.harpercollinschildrens.com

Library of Congress Control Number: 2023943869
ISBN 978-0-06-325720-7 (pbk bdg) — ISBN 978-0-06-325721-4 (trade bdg)

Typography by Laura Mock
24 25 26 27 28 PC/CWR 10 9 8 7 6 5 4 3 2 1

First Edition

Contents

Noooooooooooooo!

My name is A.J., and I know what you're thinking. You're thinking about cars with toilets. I know because that's what *I'm* thinking about.

Why don't they put toilets in cars? If they put a toilet in every car, you wouldn't have to drive around searching for a bathroom every time you need to go.

That's a genius idea! No wonder I'm in the gifted and talented program.

My point is, it was Friday, and it was the last day of school. Or as I call it, THE GREATEST DAY IN THE HISTORY OF THE WORLD! I couldn't stop smiling as I cleaned out my desk and got ready for the dismissal bell.

Brrrrrrrriiiiiinnnnnnggggg!

"YAY!" That's also "YAY" backward. My friends Ryan and Michael and I started singing that old song "School's . . . out . . . for . . . summer!" YouTube it.

But as soon as I got home, my parents dropped the hammer on me.

"We have great news, A.J.," they said.

Uh-oh. Any time your parents say they have great news, you *know* something horrible is about to happen. That's the first rule of grown-ups.

"You're having a baby?" I asked.

My parents laughed even though I didn't say anything funny.

"No," said my dad. "This summer, we're sending you to sleepaway camp."

What?! Noooooooooooooo!

Back in ancient times when dinosaurs roamed the earth, both of my parents went to sleepaway camp. They're always talking about how much they loved going to camp during the summer.

Mom: Remember making s'mores around the campfire, honey?

Dad: And hiking in the woods!

Mom: And swimming! And playing sports!

Dad: The great outdoors!

Mom: And making friendships that last a lifetime!

Dad: And learning survival skills.

Such great memories!

Mom: And these days they probably have pickleball!

"Summer camp was where we first met and fell in love," said my dad. "Remember, dear?"

"Of course I do!"

Then they started smooching and getting all lovey-dovey. *Gross.* Smooching should be illegal.

"I don't *want* to go to sleepaway camp," I insisted.

"Well," my dad said, "what *do* you want to do over summer vacation?"

"I want to play video games and watch TV," I replied.

"You do that *every* day, A.J.," said my

mom. "You spend *way* too much time staring at screens as it is. You need to be outside, in the fresh air."

"We could bring the TV outside," I said hopefully.

"No!" shouted both my parents.

"How about sending me to Antarctica for the summer?" I asked. "I'll go live with the penguins. *That* would be outside."

"We're *not* sending you to Antarctica," my dad said firmly.

"It's just a week, sweetie," said my mom. "You'll have fun!"

"A week is *seven* days!" I protested.* "I

---

*Because seven days seems a lot longer than a week. Nobody knows why.

want to stay home and be with my friends."

"We already talked with your friends' parents," my mom told me. "Michael is going to sleepaway camp. So is Ryan. Neil will be there too. *All* your friends will be there."

I didn't care *who's* gonna be there. This was sure to be the worst summer in the history of summers.

Camp
Ahdoanwanna

On Sunday, we drove a million hundred miles until there weren't any houses or stores on the side of the road anymore. This dumb sleepaway camp was in the middle of nowhere.

Or maybe it was in the edge of nowhere. How can nowhere have a middle? My point is, there was nothing around. If a spaceship landed in the road and some aliens kidnapped us, nobody would know about it.

"I gotta pee," I told my parents.

"Is it an emergency, A.J.?" asked my mom. "We'll be at the camp any minute."

Man, they should *really* put toilets in cars. Toilets should be like seatbelts.

Finally, we came to a sign at the side of the road—CAMP AHDOANWANNA. We had to drive a long way on a dusty dirt road through the woods until we reached the camp.

You know who *really* loves going to sleepaway camp? Mosquitoes! As soon as

I got out of the car, I was attacked by a swarm of them. They were all over the place.

That was weird. Mosquitoes can go anywhere they want. Why do they all go to sleepaway camp?

A golf cart came zipping down the dirt road and stopped in front of us. Some old guy with a beard hopped out. His T-shirt said "Camp Ahdoanwanna" on it.

"Welcome!" he said, pumping my hand, "I'm Uncle Ahdoanwanna, the director of Camp Ahdoanwanna! Are you ready to have fun, fun, fun?"

"No, no, no," I replied.

"Ha-ha-ha!" he laughed. "Kids always

say that. But I promise you, six days from now, you'll be crying your eyes out because you won't want to go home."

"I really doubt that," I told him.

Uncle Ahdoanwanna checked his clipboard for my name. Then he showed me which bunk I should go to. It was right next to the big flagpole in the middle

of all the bunks. I dragged my duffel bag out of the car while my parents talked to Uncle Ahdoanwanna about the weather and other stuff grown-ups care about.

Some kids were hanging out on the front porch of the bunk. As I got closer, I saw Michael, Ryan, Neil, and a boy I didn't know.

"I didn't know you guys wanted to go to sleepaway camp," I told my friends.

"I only came because my parents said *you* would be here," Michael said to Ryan.

"I only came because my parents said *you* would be here," Ryan said to Michael.

"I only came because my parents said you three would be here," said Neil.

Oh, great. *None* of us wanted to go to sleepaway camp. Our parents tricked us into going by telling us the rest of us would be going.*

Mom and Dad came over to me to say goodbye.

"Well, this is it," said my dad. "You're going to have a great time, A.J. We'll see you on Saturday."

"You be a good boy," said my mom, giving me a hug.

"No hugging in front of the guys!" I told her.

---

*Well played, parents.

"We love you, A.J.," said my dad.

Not the L word! Gross!

"I can't believe it," my mom said with tears in her eyes. "Look at you, such a big boy going to sleepaway camp. It seems like only yesterday that you were in diapers."

Then they drove away.

"You were in diapers yesterday?" Ryan asked. The guys all laughed even though he didn't say anything funny.

I dragged my duffel bag into the bunk. There were mosquitoes in there too. I could already feel the bites on my arms and legs.

Everything inside the bunk was made out of wood. It was like Abraham Lincoln's house. The one kid I didn't know followed me inside.

"Psssssssst!" he whispered. "C'mere."

I went over to him. He was wearing a trench coat, like spies wear. What is his problem? Who wears a trench coat during the summer?

"You new?" he whispered.

"Yeah," I told him.

"Well, I've been coming to this camp since I was six," he whispered. "I know all the ins and outs. What's your name?"

"A.J.," I told him. "What's yours?"

"Shhhhh!" he whispered, for no reason. "Everybody calls me . . . Candyman."

"Why do they call you Candyman?" I

asked Candyman.

He opened his trench coat. All kinds of candy were hanging from it. Kit Kats. Milk Duds. Sugar Babies. Twix. Snickers. Mars bars. It was like his trench coat was a candy store.

"You like candy?" he whispered. "I'm your man. I'll set you up. I've got gummy

bears, jawbreakers, Skittles, whatever you need. Just don't tell anybody. It will be our little secret."

"Maybe later," I replied.

That Candyman kid is weird. My parents always tell me not to take candy from strangers, and this kid was stranger than anybody.

I looked around. There were bunk beds in the bunk, of course. I guess that's why they're called bunk beds. If I picked a top bunk, I might roll over and fall out of bed in the middle of the night. And if I picked a bottom bunk, some kid in the top bunk might roll over, fall out of bed in the middle of the night, and land on top of me. I didn't know which was worse.

It didn't matter because, by the time I got there, there was only one empty bed left. I started to unpack my stuff. That's when Ryan, Michael, and Neil came in from the porch. They were with some tall, skinny teenager.

"Gather around, Owls," he told us.

"Owls?"

"Every bunk has a name," the teenager said. "It's a camp tradition. We're the Owls."

"Are you our counselor?" I asked him.

"No, Einstein," he replied. "I'm Santa Claus."

I think that's called sarcasm. That's when somebody says mean stuff to make you look dumb. Teenagers are sarcastic all the time. I hope I never become a teenager.

The counselor said we should call him Uncle Ray. All the guys who work at Camp Ahdoanwanna are called uncle even if

they're not your uncle. Nobody knows why. I guess it's another camp tradition.

"You boys are going to remember this summer for the rest of your lives," said Uncle Ray. "You know why?"

"No, why?"

"Because it's gonna be horrible!" Uncle Ray replied. "There are bugs everywhere. It's hot, dirty, and smelly. You'll probably get hurt. You'll make enemies that will last a lifetime. If you're lucky, you'll get food poisoning so you can go home early."

Camp sounded *terrible*.

"So why are *you* here?" Ryan asked Uncle Ray.

"I got bad grades in school," he explained. "My parents are punishing me by forcing me to take care of you twerps."

Uncle Ray was a real downer.

"Let's go over the rules," he said. "Rule number one—no candy in the bunk. It attracts bugs and mice and other non-human creatures."

I shot a look at Candyman, and he winked at me.

"The bugs are already in here," muttered Michael.

"Hey, I don't make the rules," said Uncle Ray. "Rule number two—lights out at nine o'clock sharp."

What?! At home, I get to stay up late

during the summer.

"Rule number three," Uncle Ray said. "Every morning before breakfast, we clean up the bunk. There's a chore wheel on the wall by the door."

What?!

"We have to *clean*?"

"I don't have to clean at home!"

"It's not fair!"

We were all whining.

"Rule number four," Uncle Ray said. "No whining."

Oh, man! If you ask me, Camp Ahdoanwanna should be called Camp Jail.

"Finally," said Uncle Ray, "you need to learn the Owl bunk cheer. Repeat after me.

Hoot, hoot, hoot! We don't give a hoot!"

"HOOT, HOOT, HOOT! WE DON'T GIVE A HOOT!" we all yelled, even though the cheer is totally lame.

"If you have any questions," said Uncle Ray, "Ahdoanwanna hear 'em."

"What's that stuff hanging from the ceiling?" Neil asked.

I looked up. There were strips of yellow paper dangling down from the rafters.

"That's flypaper," said Uncle Ray. "It's coated with sticky poison, so flies stick to it and die. We also have bees, ants, mice, bats, spiders, skunks, and snakes."

Snakes?! Everybody was freaking out.

"Don't worry," said Uncle Ray. "If you

get bitten by a snake and you die, your parents get some of their money back."

"Do we ever get to have any fun?" asked Neil.

"Yeah," said Uncle Ray. "Six days from now. When you go home."

I remembered that I never got the chance to pee on the drive to camp. Now I really had to go.

"Where's the bathroom?" I asked, looking around the bunk.

"It's in the woods, down the road," said Uncle Ray. "Just make a left at the rock that looks like a bear. Then make a right at the bear that looks like a rock. You can't miss it."

"Where's the TV?" Neil asked.

"In your dreams," replied Uncle Ray. "Look, it's a *camp*. We don't have a bathroom and we don't have a TV. You know what *else* we don't have?"

"What?" we all asked.

"Parents!" he replied. "So look on the bright side."

Hmmmm. I've never been away from my parents for a week. Maybe sleepaway camp wouldn't be so bad.

Go Jump in a Lake

3

"It's time for swimming!" announced Uncle Ray.

YAY! I love swimming. I can swim better than anybody. One time, I swam across the Pacific Ocean.

Okay, I made that up.

It looked like it was going to start

raining, but we all put on our bathing suits and flip-flops. Then we walked a million hundred miles through the woods. Uncle Ray let us stop off at the bathroom. I had even more mosquito bites than I thought. Those mosquitoes must *love* me.

"Where's the pool?" I asked as we marched through the woods.

"Pool?" Uncle Ray replied with a snort. "Do you think this is a country club? We swim in the lake."

Lake?

I never swam in a lake before. Lakes are for fishing. Lakes have mud and rocks and all kinds of gross stuff in them.

Finally, we reached the lake. There was

a long wooden dock going out into the water and a smaller dock floating in the middle. A lifeguard with big muscles came over to us. I knew he was the lifeguard because he had a whistle around his neck. Also, he was wearing a tank top that said LIFEGUARD on it.

"Welcome to Lake Ahdoanwanna, Owls," he said. "I'm Uncle Craig. How many of you dudes already know how to swim?"

Everybody raised a hand. Uncle Craig said we'd have to pass a deep-water test to prove we were good swimmers. We would have to swim out to the floating dock, tread water for sixty seconds, and then swim back.

"It will be a piece of cake," said Uncle Craig.

Huh? What did cake have to do with anything? Maybe he was going to give us

cake if we passed the swimming test.

It was starting to drizzle, but Uncle Craig didn't seem to care. He had us line up on the dock. There were lots of mosquitoes flitting around. Of course. At least when I'm underwater, I figured, the mosquitoes can't bite me.

"We have to swim in the rain?" Michael asked.

"What's the matter, dude?" asked Uncle Craig. "Are you afraid you'll get wet? Ha-ha-ha!"

He laughed like that was the funniest joke in the history of jokes.

"All right!" he continued. "Let's go. Ready, Owls?"

"HOOT, HOOT, HOOT! WE DON'T

GIVE A HOOT!" we all yelled.

Uncle Craig blew his whistle. Ryan jumped in the water, swam out to the dock, treaded water for sixty seconds, and swam back.

"Good job, dude!" hollered Uncle Craig. He blew his whistle.

Michael jumped in, swam out to the dock, treaded water for sixty seconds, and swam back.

"Nice form, dude!" hollered Uncle Craig, who definitely says the word "dude" too much. He blew his whistle again.

Neil jumped in, swam out to the dock, treaded water for sixty seconds, and swam back.

"Beautiful, dude!" hollered Uncle Craig.

He blew his whistle again.

It was my turn. I jumped in and started swimming. I swam out to the dock and started treading water. I counted ten seconds in my head. Twenty seconds. Thirty seconds.

Man, lake water is *dirty*! It's probably filled with plankton and bacteria and algae and other slimy stuff.

Forty seconds.

I felt something touch my foot while I was treading water. Was that a fish?

Fifty seconds.

A fish was nibbling at my toes! Or maybe it was a whole *school* of fish! Gross! I don't mind eating fish, but I don't want them eating *me*.

Sixty seconds. Time to start swimming back to the dock.

While I was trying to get my feet away from the fish, my mouth slipped under for a moment and I swallowed a little water.

Ugh. Dirty, disgusting lake water! That's when I realized something.

Fish pee in lakes!

I swallowed fish pee!

I was freaking out.

Glub, glub.

I don't know what happened after that. I don't know how much time had passed. All I knew was that I was lying on my back on the dock and somebody was blowing air into my mouth. I opened my eyes.

And you'll never believe in a million

hundred years who was giving me mouth-to-mouth resuscitation.

I'm not going to tell you.

Okay, okay, I'll tell you.

It was Andrea Young, this girl in my class at school with curly brown hair!*

Noooooooooooooo!

"Ooooh," said Ryan. "A.J. and Andrea are kissing! They must be in *love!*"

"When are you gonna get married?" asked Michael.

I jumped up. Andrea was wearing pink sunglasses and a bathing suit with butter-flies on it. A few other girls were behind her.

---

*Well, the school doesn't have curly brown hair. Andrea does.

"Ugh, gross! Disgusting!" I said as I wiped my mouth.

"I saved your life, Arlo!" said Andrea, who calls me by my real name because she knows I don't like it. "And this is the thanks I get?"

"What are *you* doing here?" I demanded.

"I go to Camp Botshagotta," Andrea said. "It's on the other side of the lake."

"I dragged you out of the water," said Uncle Craig. "You were drowning, dude."

"Then why didn't *you* give me mouth-to-mouth resuscitation?" I asked him.

"This young lady volunteered," he explained. "She said she took a CPR class after school."

Of course. Andrea takes classes in *everything* after school. If they gave classes in clipping your toenails, she would take that class so she could get better at it.

I changed my mind. This was going to be the worst summer in the history of summers.

The Mess Hall

After my humiliation at the lake, we changed into our clothes and walked to the dining hall, which everybody calls the mess hall. When I walked in, the first thing I saw was a giant moose head sticking out over the door. That was weird.

"What's with the moose head?" I asked Candyman.

"Anybody who gets a care package in the mail has to kiss the moose," he told me.

"Why?"

"It's a camp tradition," he explained as he picked some spoons out of the silverware tray and put them in the pocket of his trench coat.

"Why are you stealing spoons?" I asked.

"I can't take it anymore," he whispered. "So I'm gonna tunnel out of this joint. *Shhhh!* Don't tell anybody."

"You're going to dig a tunnel with *spoons*?" I asked.

"Yeah," he replied. "In the middle of the night. You wanna help?"

"Uh, maybe some other time," I replied. That guy is weird.

It was really noisy in the dining hall. After I found a seat at the Owl table, Uncle Ahdoanwanna came in. He clapped his hands and shouted, "I would like to make an announcement!"

"ANNOUNCEMENTS! ANNOUNCE-MENTS! ANNOUNCEMENTS!" everybody chanted.

"This afternoon," announced Uncle Ahdoanwanna, "we will have softball, basketball, and pickleball. And tonight will be a campfire in the woods."

"YAY!" everybody shouted. "Ahdoan-wanna! Youdoanwanna! Wedoanwanna! Theydoanwanna!"

"Okay, let's eat!" shouted Uncle Ahdoan-wanna.

The Owl table went up to the window to get our food. There was a lady behind the counter wearing a yellow hat, yellow shirt, yellow pants, and yellow gloves.

"I'm Aunt Kim," she told us. "Are you boys hungry for lunch?"

"I'm starving!" I replied. "Do you have hamburgers?"

"No," she said.

"Hot dogs?" I asked.

"Sorry, no."

"Uh, chicken strips?"

"Sorry."

"How about a peanut butter and jelly sandwich?" I asked. She would *have* to have *that*.

"Today is Yellow Day at Camp Ahdoanwanna," she said. "All the food is yellow."

Huh? That was weird. It must be another one of those camp traditions. I guess you can explain *anything* that makes no sense by calling it a tradition.

"Do you like mac and cheese?" Aunt Kim asked me.

"No," I said. "I can't stand mac and cheese."

"No problem," she replied. "We have lots of other choices. Do you like corn on the cob?"

"Not really," I replied.

"We also have hard-boiled egg yolks, pineapples, lemons, and yellow oatmeal."

Yellow oatmeal?

"I'll have the mac and cheese," I told her.

"Good choice!" she said, putting a big glop of the stuff on a plate. "Want more?

It's all you can eat."

"I don't want to eat *any* of it," I said.

"How about a tall glass of yellow bug juice?" she asked.

Oh, man. They have so many bugs here that they put them in the juice.

"Can I have juice *without* bugs in it?" I asked.

"Sorry," she replied, "it's impossible to remove the bugs. I can give you *extra* bugs if you'd like."

"I'll just have water," I told her.

"Lake water?"

"No!"

I brought my tray to the Owl table. Ryan was eating yellow oatmeal, which looked totally gross. But then, Ryan will eat *any-thing*. He had an empty glass in front of him. While he ate, he started putting stuff in the glass—ketchup. Mustard. Mayonnaise. Salt. Pepper.

"What are you doing?" I asked him.

"I'm inventing a new drink," Ryan replied as he mixed it up with a spoon.

Ugh. Now I know why they call it the mess hall. We all agreed that Ryan's drink looked gross.

"That's probably what they said about Mr. Pepsi when he invented Pepsi," Ryan said.* "What's the big deal? These are all

---

*I really doubt that Pepsi was invented by a guy named Mr. Pepsi.

ingredients you eat anyway."

That made sense, I guess. I do like ketchup and mustard and all that other stuff. But still, his drink looked totally disgusting.

"Hey, A.J.," said Michael. "I'll give you a quarter if you drink that."

"I'm not drinking that," I told him.

"What if I gave you two quarters?" asked Michael.

"No way," I said.

"I'll give you a *dollar* to drink it," said Neil.

"Thanks, but no thanks," I replied.

"I'll give you *five* dollars," said Candy-man.

Hmmmm. Five dollars is a lot of money.

"You mean all I have to do is take a sip?" I asked.

"No," Candyman replied. "You have to drink the whole thing."

I looked at the glass. Ugh.

"Would you give me *ten* dollars?" I asked.

"I think it's worth ten dollars to watch A.J. drink that," said Candyman.

"DRINK IT! DRINK IT! DRINK IT!" all the Owls chanted.

Everybody in the mess hall started banging on their tables, stomping their feet, and chanting, "DRINK IT!"

"For ten dollars?" I said. "Okay, I'll drink it."

"YAY!"

Everyone was looking at me.

I picked up the glass.

I closed my eyes.

I brought the glass up to my lips.

I tilted my head back.

And I drank it. The whole thing. Ugh. It was horrible. I thought I was gonna die. But I did it. I put the empty glass down and let out a nasty burp.

"Okay, I drank it," I told Candyman. "Give me ten dollars."

"I don't have any money," he replied.

WHAT?!

I wanted to yell at him or something, but I didn't have the chance because Uncle Ahdoanwanna got up and said he had another announcement.

"ANNOUNCEMENTS! ANNOUNCE-MENTS! ANNOUNCEMENTS!" everybody chanted.

"We have one care package today," announced Uncle Ahdoanwanna as he held up a box. "It's for someone in the Owl cabin . . . named . . . A.J.!"

A care package for *me*? Wow, I guess my

parents must have mailed it a few days before camp started.

"He has to kiss the moose!" somebody shouted.

"I don't want to kiss the moose," I said.

"You have to," said Candyman. "It's the tradition."

Everybody started banging on their tables, stomping their feet, and chanting, "KISS THE MOOSE! KISS THE MOOSE! KISS THE MOOSE!"

So I stood up.

Somebody brought a ladder under the moose head.

I climbed the ladder.

And I kissed the moose.

I thought I was gonna throw up. This was the worst day of my life. I wanted to run away to Antarctica and live with the penguins. Penguins don't have to kiss a moose. Or mooses. Or meese.

Rest Hour Is Boring

Before we could leave the mess hall, the counselors made us scrape off our plates and put them on a long conveyor belt that went into the kitchen. Candyman told me there are a bunch of Oompa-Loompas from *Charlie and the Chocolate Factory* back there who wash the dishes, but I'm not sure if he just made that up.

"Follow me, Owls!" said Uncle Ray.

We went back to our bunk and I opened my care package. And you'll never believe what was inside it.

Candy!

Yay! I have the best parents in the world.

Too bad my stomach was upset from drinking Ryan's gross drink in the mess hall. I love candy, but just the thought of it now made me want to throw up. Uncle Ray said the candy would attract bugs, and I had to eat it right away or get rid of it. So I gave all the candy to my bunkmates.

It wasn't fair! I had to drink that horrible drink and kiss a dead moose head, but

I couldn't eat my own candy.* Bummer in the summer!

Uncle Ray said it was rest hour. We had to stay on our beds the whole time. Yeah, like we were babies.

"I'm not tired," I told him.

"Too bad," he replied. Then he lay down on his bed and fell asleep.

Rest hour is boring. There was nothing to do. Michael was playing solitaire. Ryan was eating my candy. Neil was reading a book. Candyman found a little hole in the floorboard under his bed, and he was trying to dig a tunnel with a spoon.

I started writing a letter . . .

---

*And I never even got my ten dollars.

Dear Mom and Dad,

This place is horrible. I have 39 mosquito bites. I mean 40. I just got another one. Ryan played connect the dots on my back, and it made a picture that looks like the Big Dipper. I had to drink a horrible drink with ketchup and mustard in it. Then I had to kiss a dead moose. And that's just the first day! I want to come home! Can you pick me up ASAP? If I have to spend another hour here, I'm—

I didn't have the chance to finish my letter because the weirdest thing in the history of the world happened.

"EEEEEEEEEKKKKKK!"

It was Neil, screaming.

"What's the matter?" Ryan asked.

"There's a daddy longlegs on my bed!" Neil shouted.

Gross! Spiders are yucky. I'm glad it wasn't on my bed.

Uncle Ray jumped up off his bed when he heard Neil scream.

"What's going on?" he asked.

"There's a daddy longlegs on my bed," said Neil. "I'm afraid."

Uncle Ray just laughed.

"Spiders are nothing to be afraid of," he told Neil. "They're part of nature. Tell you what. Let's give the spider a name. If we name any spiders we find in our bunk, it will make them less scary."

Hmmmm. I had to admit it. That was

pretty smart. I wouldn't give Uncle Ray the Nobel Prize or anything, but he did have a good idea.

"Let's call this one Henry," said Uncle Ray, flicking the spider off Neil's bed. "See, now he's not so scary."

Neil calmed down. I went back to writing my letter home. I was almost finished when I felt a funny feeling on the back of my neck. I thought it was another mosquito bite.

"Dude," said Ryan, "I think Henry is on you."

"He's crawling up your head!" Michael shouted.

"EEEEEEEEEK!" I screamed.

"Kill him!" everybody was shouting. "Kill him!"

So I whacked Henry with a sneaker. And that was the end of Henry.

Lights Out

Torture hour, I mean rest hour, was over. I felt bad for Henry the spider, after we had given him a name and all. Everybody felt bad. So we held a little funeral. Candyman dug a hole with a spoon, and we buried him next to the bunk.

We buried Henry, that is. Of course we didn't bury Candyman.

Our bunk was scheduled to play pickle-ball in the afternoon, but it was raining, so all outdoor activities were canceled. Instead, we had arts and crafts. Or as everybody calls it, arts and farts.

You should always call arts and crafts arts and farts. That's the first rule of being a kid.

"Welcome to the arts and crafts room," said the arts and farts counselor. "I'm Aunt Nancy. Today, we're going to use rubber bands to make friendship bracelets for each other. Doesn't that sound like fun?"

"No!" we all shouted.

"I'm not making a friendship bracelet," I announced.

"Me neither," said Ryan.

"No way," said Michael.

"Friendship bracelets are for girls," said Neil.

"Yeah!" we all shouted.

We crossed our arms in front of our chests. That's what you do to let grown-ups know you're not going to do something.

"Oh, did I say friendship bracelets?" asked Aunt Nancy. "I'm sorry. I meant to say we're going to make *man bands*."

Well, *that's* different.

Man bands are cool, and they show everybody that you're a guy. Each of us made a man band, and then Aunt Nancy said we could pass them around to our friends if we wanted to. I gave my man band to Ryan. Ryan gave his man band to Michael. Michael gave his man band to Neil. Neil gave his man band to me. Candyman just kept his man band.

After that, we went to the mess hall for dinner, where we ate some disgusting yellow food that I couldn't identify. The evening activity was some dumb movie about rabbits. Then we went back to the bunk.

"Okay, brush your teeth and put your pj's on," said Uncle Ray. "Lights out in fifteen minutes."

"What?" I shouted. "It's still daytime!"

"We have a big day ahead of us tomorrow," said Uncle Ray.

"But it's too early to go to bed!" complained Ryan.

It wasn't fair. I told Uncle Ray that I get to stay up as late as I want when I'm at home. That wasn't exactly true, but I thought it might help us win the argument.

It didn't. Uncle Ray flipped off the light and told us he was going to play Ping-Pong with the other counselors in the

aunts' and uncles' lounge.

"Good night, Owls!" he said. "No talking." Then he left.

I lay there for a few minutes, trying to fall asleep.

"Pssssst!" a voice *psssst*ed at me. It was Candyman. "A.J., do you want some candy? I've got plenty."

"No thanks," I whispered.

"Hey," he whispered, "did you hear about the demon drone that hovers over the camp at night?"

"I'm trying to sleep," I whispered.

"He's got laser eyes that can see through walls," Candyman continued. "As soon as you fall asleep, he floats down and—"

"Will you give it a rest?" I whispered.

It was quiet for a minute or two.

"Hey, let's tell ghost stories," whispered Neil.

"Yeah!" somebody whispered.

"I got a great one," whispered Michael. "There was this ghost . . ."

"Yeah . . ."

"And he was dead," whispered Michael.

"*All* ghosts are dead," I whispered.

"So this dead ghost gets lost in the middle of the woods," whispered Michael. "And he walks into a sleepaway camp."

"Yeah?" I asked. "Then what happened?"

"Uh . . ." said Michael, "the ghost killed everybody."

"That ghost story was lame, dude," I told Michael.

Ryan told a story about a ghost who eats aluminum foil and turns into a jet plane. Neil told a story about a ghost who eats kids, but only kids who are left-handed. We were making up scary ghost stories late into the night.

Finally, at some point, I fell asleep. That's when the weirdest thing in the history of the world happened. But I'm not going to tell you what it was.

Okay, okay, I'll tell you.

It was pitch-dark, so I couldn't see anything. But I heard a noise. It sounded like fingernails on the floor next to my bed. I didn't think anything of it at first. But then, there was this soft grunting noise. I reached for my flashlight. I turned it on and pointed the beam at the floor. That's when I saw it.

"THERE'S A SKUNK IN THE BUNK!" I shouted.*

Well *that* woke everybody up.

"Eeeeeeeek!" somebody screamed.

"What's going on?" Ryan asked groggily.

"THERE'S A SKUNK IN THE BUNK!"

Everybody was yelling and screaming and hooting and hollering and freaking out. The other guys got out flashlights and shined them all over the place.

"Where did it go?" somebody shouted.

"Help!" yelled Neil. "I think the skunk touched me!"

---

*Hey, that would make a good book title!

"I want my mommy!" somebody shouted.

"This is *your* fault, Candyman!" I shouted. "They told us not to keep candy in the bunk! Now we have a skunk in here! He probably came out of that hole under your bed!"

"Never mind that!" shouted Ryan. "Where's the skunk?"

"We should name the skunk so it won't be scary!" Neil shouted.

"Get a broom!" Michael shouted.

"Open the door so it can run out!" shouted Neil.

"If we open the door, ten more skunks might run in!" shouted Ryan.

It was crazy. We chased the skunk around the bunk in the dark with tennis rackets and baseball bats. Everybody was tripping over the beds and crashing into each other. You should have been there!

Finally, the skunk ran out the door.

Unhappy Campers

After we chased the skunk out of the bunk, it was hard to fall asleep again. My heart was racing. I think I got about twenty minutes of sleep all night. The first thing I heard on Monday morning was . . .

"RISE AND SHINE!"

It was Uncle Ahdoanwanna, the camp director.

"Everybody up!" he shouted as he threw open the door to our bunk. "The rain stopped! The sun is out! It's a perfect day for hiking!"

Oh no. Not hiking.

"Do we *have* to?" I groaned.

"Yes!" he replied, all excited. "We're going on a ten-mile hike."

What?! We have to walk *ten miles*? Didn't they invent cars so people wouldn't have to walk ten miles?

We got dressed. Uncle Ahdoanwanna told us to put on bug spray and sunscreen, and to fill our water bottles.

"Hydrate or die-drate!" he shouted.

"What about breakfast?" Neil asked.

Uncle Ahdoanwanna tossed each of us

a granola bar and said, "Here's your break-fast. Let's go!"

We followed him on a path that led to the woods behind the camp.

"If we're lucky," Uncle Ahdoanwanna said, "maybe we'll see some wildlife."

Wildlife? We didn't have to go on a hike to see wildlife. It was in our bunk last night.

We started walking. And walking. And walking. My feet were hurting. My back was sore. My legs were itchy all over.

"Are we there yet?" asked Ryan.

"Isn't there a bus we can take?" asked Neil.

Uncle Ahdoanwanna laughed. "Look at that tree!" he said, pointing at some dumb tree. "It's a pignut hickory."

I say if you've seen one tree, you've seen 'em all. But Uncle Ahdoanwanna had to point out every tree, fern, and bush we passed along the way. What a snoozefest.

My feet hurt. I had mosquito bites all over my body.* I thought I was gonna die.

"Look!" Uncle Ahdoan-wanna shouted sud-denly and pointed at the

---

*I think bug spray must *attract* bugs.

ground in front of us. "It's a banana slug!"

If you don't know what a banana slug is, you're not missing much. It's a slug that looks like a banana. So it has the perfect name. It's even yellow. I'm surprised they didn't serve it for lunch in the mess hall.

"They say it brings good luck if you kiss a banana slug," said Uncle Ahdoanwanna.

"A.J.," said Ryan, "you should kiss the banana slug."

"Forget it," I replied.

"KISS THE SLUG! KISS THE SLUG!" everybody started chanting.

I don't care how much they chant. I'm not kissing a slug.

We walked a million hundred miles through the woods. At some point, Candyman sidled up to me.

"Y'know," he whispered, "if we had tunneled out of camp last night, we wouldn't be doing this right now."

"Yeah?" I replied. "Well, soon my parents will get the letter I wrote them, and they'll take me home. I'll be out of here."

Finally, there was a clearing in the woods, and I could see Camp Ahdoanwanna. We must have walked ten miles in a big circle. In other words, we didn't go *anywhere*. What a waste of time.

"Wasn't that fun?" asked Uncle Ahdoanwanna.

"No!" we all shouted.

Before he left us, I saw him looking at my leg.

"Hmmmm," he said, "you might have poison ivy, A.J. I need to take you to the infirmary."

I've never had poison ivy before, but it sounds horrible because it has the word "poison" in it. Uncle Ahdoanwanna led us to a cabin that said INFIRMARY on the door. There was a lady inside.

"Hi, everybody!" she said. "I'm Aunt Debbie, the camp nurse. What's the problem?"

"A.J. has poison ivy," said Michael.

Aunt Debbie looked at my leg and said *"Hmmmm"* over and over again. And do you know what she did next?

She put a Band-Aid on my leg.

What?!

"Do you have any medicine?" I asked.

"Oh, I'm not allowed to give out medicine," said Aunt Debbie.

In the corner was a box of Band-Aids the size of a mailbox. She must give out Band-Aids for *everything*. So I guess if you fall off a cliff and break every bone in your body, Aunt Debbie would give you a Band-Aid.

No way that lady is a real nurse. She probably kidnapped the real nurse and tied her up in an underground

bunker somewhere. That stuff happens all the time.

"As long as you're here," said Aunt Debbie, "we should do a tick check."

"I don't have a watch," I said.

"Not *that* kind of tick, dumbhead!" said Neil.

A tick check, I found out, is when the nurse checks to make sure you don't have ticks. So it has the perfect name.

Aunt Debbie looked us over carefully. Nobody had ticks. Then she said she wanted to check us for head lice.

"Why would we have headlights?" I asked. "We're not cars."

"Not headlights, dumbhead! Head lice!"

Oh. I knew that.

The Indoor Olympics

We were supposed to have archery out in the field, but it rained.

We were supposed to go rock climbing, but it rained.

We were supposed to play pickleball, but it rained.

It rained *all the time*! On Tuesday and

Wednesday, there were no outdoor activities. Instead, they had us do something called the Indoor Olympics.

The Lame Games is more like it.

First we had to play a game called Balloon Baseball. You hit a balloon up in the air, and then you have to run around the bases while the other team tries to keep the balloon in the air by blowing on it with straws.

That game was lame.

Then we played a game called Hot Seat. You sit in a chair, and one kid holds a piece of paper behind your head with a word on it. Everybody gives you clues to help you guess what the word is.

That game was lame.

Then we played a game called Musical Baby Food. You stand in a circle and pass around a spoon while music plays. When the music stops, whoever is holding the spoon has to eat a spoonful of baby food from a jar.

That game was lame too. We played all kinds of lame games. It was like the counselors were desperate to come up with indoor activities so we wouldn't notice it was raining all the time. What a snooze-fest. I just hoped my parents got my letter and would pick me up soon.

"Okay, that was fun!" exclaimed Uncle Ahdoanwanna after the last game in the Indoor Olympics. "Our next game . . . "

Ugh. Not another one.

". . . is called Guess Who's in the Sleeping Bag?"

That's a weird name for a game. But it was also the perfect name for the game because four counselors carried in a big, lumpy sleeping bag and rested it on the floor.

"Okay, this game is easy to play," said Uncle Ahdoanwanna. "All you have to do is guess who's in the sleeping bag."

I looked at the sleeping bag. It was all zipped up. There was no way to tell who was inside it.

"Is it Uncle Ray?" I asked.

"No . . . " said Uncle Ahdoanwanna.

"Is it Aunt Kim?" asked Michael.

"No . . . "

"Is it Uncle Craig, the swimming counselor?" asked Ryan.

"No . . . "

"Is it Aunt Nancy?" asked Candyman.

"No . . . "

"Can you give us a hint?" asked Neil.

"You fellas need to think outside the box," said Uncle Ahdoanwanna.*

"Is it George Washington?" asked Neil.

"George Washington is dead, dumbhead," said Michael.

"Hey, there could be a dead guy in there," Neil replied.

---

*What did boxes have to do with anything? The person was in a sleeping bag, not a box.

Good point. Whoever was inside the sleeping bag hadn't moved at all.

"I'm . . . not . . . dead," said a voice from inside the sleeping bag.

We all just about jumped out of our skin. But the voice was familiar. I know I had heard it somewhere before.

"We give up," Ryan finally said. "Who's in the sleeping bag?"

Uncle Ahdoanwanna unzipped the zipper. And you'll never believe in a million hundred years who was inside the sleeping bag.

I'm not going to tell you.

Okay, okay, I'll tell you.

It was our old principal from Ella Mentry

School, Mr. Klutz!

He has no hair at all. He must need a lot of sunscreen in the summer so his head doesn't burn. Mr. Klutz was our principal until he retired last year.

"Mr. Klutz!" I shouted. "What are *you* doing here?"

"I missed you boys!" he said, hugging us all. "Uncle Ahdoanwanna is a good friend of mine. He asked me if I would like to visit the camp, and I said sure. I used to go to camp here. Believe it or not, I was a boy once."

"Just once?" I asked. "I'm a boy all the time."

Guess Who's in the Sleeping Bag was a fun game, but we were all bored out of our minds. During dinner in the mess hall, we were trying to think of something to do.

"Y'know what we should do?"

Candyman suggested. "We should put a goat in Uncle Ahdoanwanna's cabin. That would be funny."

"Where are we going to get a goat?" asked Ryan.

"From Rent-A-Goat," I told him. "You can rent anything. Hey, y'know what we should do? We should sneak over to the girls' camp in the middle of the night and scare them."

"No, we should do a panty raid," suggested Neil.

"What's that?" Michael asked.

"That's when you steal somebody's underwear," Neil explained. "Then we could bring it back to our camp and run it up the flagpole."

"That would be hilarious," said Ryan.

"The girls' camp is all the way on the other side of the lake," said Michael.

"We'd never get away with it," said Candyman. "We would have to get past the counselors on guard duty."

We decided that sneaking over to the girls' camp to steal underwear was a dumb idea. We'd just have to play more boring indoor games until the rain stopped.

But after dinner, the most amazing thing in the history of the world happened. I'm not going to tell you what it was.

Okay, okay, I'll tell you. But you have to read the next chapter. So nah-nah-nah boo-boo on you!

Good Surprises
and
Bad Surprises

"What's tonight's evening activity?" Ryan asked Uncle Ray as we scraped our dinner plates into the garbage can.

"It's a surprise," he replied.

Hmmmm. It could be a good surprise, like a pizza party or pickleball. Or it could be a not-so-good surprise, like a meteor hitting the earth and wiping out all the humans. You never know with surprises.

Uncle Ray led us to the rec hall, which is this big building behind the flagpole. It was pretty dark inside, except for some flashing lights that were shooting around like laser beams.

Cool! The evening activity was laser tag! I had a laser tag birthday party one year. It was great.

But as soon as we got in the door, I realized that we weren't going to be playing laser tag. You'll never believe in a million hundred years what was on the other side of the rec hall.

GIRLS!

NOOOOOOOOOOOO!

It looked like all the girls from Camp Botshagotta were there.

"Oh no!" said Neil.

"Let's get out of here," I said.

"We can't," said Michael, turning around. "They closed the doors behind us!"

We were trapped, like rats in a cage. I wished the surprise had been a meteor that hit the earth and wiped out all the humans.

All the girls were on one side of the rec

hall, and all the boys were on the other. Awkward! Uncle Ahdoanwanna, the camp director, walked out to the middle of the room.

"Boys and girls," he said, "welcome to the Camp Ahdoanwanna social. We're going to have a great time tonight. I'd like to introduce our guest DJ, Mr. Klutz, better known as 'The Funkmaster.'"

Mr. Klutz came running out wearing a sparkly suit that looked like it was made out of tiny mirrors. He was like a living disco ball.

Everybody clapped because that's what you do when people get introduced even though they didn't do anything yet.

"Yo! Yo! Yo!" Mr. Klutz shouted like a rapper. "It's time to get down and funky! I'm gonna drop some beats and spin the tunes you cool cats and kittens dig, you feel me? So let's cut a rug and get your groove on. Shake your booty! We're gonna party like it's 1999."

Huh? That was a long time ago. What was he talking about? Mr. Klutz is nuts.

Loud, thumping music started coming out of the speakers. Me and the guys went into a huddle, like a football team.

"He wants us to dance with those girls," said Ryan.

"What are we gonna do?" asked Neil.

"I'm not dancing," I said firmly.

"Me neither," said Michael.

The laser beams were shooting all over the place. Mr. Klutz was scratching the record on a turntable in front of him, bopping up and down to the music, and shouting into a mic.

"Come on, you guys!" yelled Mr. Klutz. "Don't be shy. The girls don't bite."

The Botshagotta girls were on the other

side of the room, giggling and whispering. It was like two armies lined up against each other before a battle.

"Maybe we should go over there and talk to them," Ryan said.

"Girls are scary," said Neil.

"I'm not going over there," I announced. "Mr. Klutz can't make us."

"Yeah, all for one and one for all," said Michael. "That's what the three muske-teers said."*

It felt like a million hundred minutes went by. Finally, Uncle Ray walked across the rec hall and went over to one of the girl counselors. He whispered something in her ear, and then the two of them

---

*Huh? What do candy bars have to do with anything?

started dancing together.

"I'm going over there," Ryan said.

"No!" I shouted. "Don't do it, Ryan!"

"A.J.," he said, putting his arm on my shoulder. "A man's gotta do what a man's gotta do."

Ryan walked over to the other side of the rec hall, went over to a girl, and the next thing we knew, the two of them were dancing.

"Look!" shouted Neil. "Ryan is dancing with a girl!"

Traitor!

The song ended, and Mr. Klutz started playing a new song. Ryan came back over to our side of the rec hall.

"How was it?" Michael asked him.

"What's that girl's name?"

"I don't know," replied Ryan. "But we're going steady. I think I'm in love."

Mr. Klutz's next song was faster and thumpier than the last one.

"I'm going over there," announced Michael.

"Wait for me," said Neil.

Noooooooooo!

Neil and Michael went over to the line of girls. They asked two of them to dance, and then the four of them were dancing in the middle of the rec hall.

One by one, the boys on our side and the girls on the other side were starting to dance with each other. I went over to the punch bowl to get a drink. Nobody was going to make *me* dance. No way.

That's when the weirdest thing in the history of the world happened. Somebody tapped me on the shoulder. I turned around.

It was Andrea Young!

Noooooooooo!

"Hi, Arlo," she said sweetly.

Oh no. Andrea was going to ask me to dance. If the guys saw me dancing with Andrea, they would make fun of me for sure. They always do.

"Are you enjoying camp so far?" Andrea asked me.

"I was until now," I replied.

"I *love* camp," said Andrea, who loves everything I hate. "What's your favorite part?"

"It will be when my parents come to pick me up," I replied.

"My favorite part is rest hour," Andrea said. "I can catch up on my summer reading. My goal is to read all the books that won the Newbery Medal."

"Great," I replied. "Listen, I gotta go."

"Go? Where?"

"Uh," I said, "I gotta go to a dentist appointment."

"There are no dentists here," Andrea said. "Do you want to dance with me, Arlo?"

"No."

"Come on," she said. "Everybody *else* is dancing. If you don't dance, your friends are going to make fun of you."

Nice try. I'm not falling for that.

"I don't know how to dance," I admitted.

"I'll show you," Andrea told me. "It's easy. You just move around to the music."

"Ask somebody else to dance with you," I said.

"Everybody else has a partner already," Andrea replied. "And besides, I want to dance with *you*. Come on. Just one dance."

I didn't know what to say. I didn't know what to do.

"Well, okay," I said, "as long as we don't have to touch each other."

"Okay."

The music was really loud and thumpy. Andrea and I started dancing. I didn't know what I was doing. I was just jumping around.

"See?" Andrea hollered. "It's fun!"

It was kind of fun, I had to admit. Then, after a few seconds, the song came to an end.

"Okay, cats and kittens," said Mr. Klutz. "We're gonna slow things down a little now. Here's a song to help you remember your week at Camp Ahdoanwanna and Camp Botshagotta.

A different song started playing.

"Memories . . . light the corners of my mind . . ."

"I love this song!" Andrea said as she put her arms around my neck.

"Hey, what are you doing?" I asked.

"It's a slow song, Arlo!" she said. "So you

have to slow dance. Put your arms around my waist."

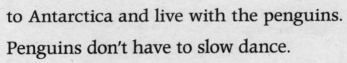

"Ahdoanwanna."

"Botshagotta."

I wanted to run away to Antarctica and live with the penguins. Penguins don't have to slow dance.

Everybody was dancing to the memory song. Soon, Ryan and his partner were on one side of us, and Michael and his partner were on our other side.

"Ooooooh," Ryan said, "A.J. is slow dancing with Andrea! They must be in *love*!"

"When are you gonna get married?" asked Michael.

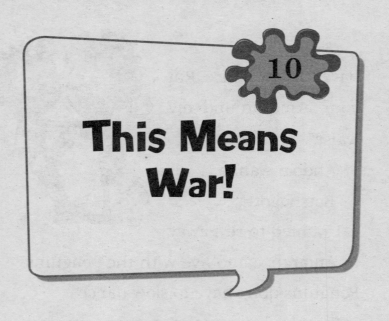

This Means War!

Well, *that* was humiliating.

On Thursday morning, it stopped raining finally. All the bunks gathered at the flagpole for assembly. Uncle Ahdoanwanna was waiting for us. He was wearing underwear over his pants. I had no idea why.

"Why are you wearing underwear on top of your clothes?" somebody asked.

"Oh," he replied. "Today is Wear Your Underwear over Your Clothes Day. I probably should have told you before you got dressed."

That was weird. Uncle Ahdoanwanna told us it was another big day too. It was Color War Day. He said we would have an all-out competition, like the Super Bowl, the World Series, and the Olympics all rolled into one.

"Who are we competing against?" somebody asked.

"Camp Botshagotta," he replied.

What?! Boys against girls?

"We will crush them!" some guy yelled, and then everybody started chanting, "CRUSH THEM! CRUSH THEM! CRUSH THEM!"

After we finished chanting, somebody hollered, "What does the winning camp get?"

"Bragging rights," said Uncle Ahdoanwanna.

Oh. In other words, you win *nothing*. Bragging rights is what you win when they don't want to give out a prize. It's not fair, but it's still fun to win.

We marched out to the big sports field that we never got to play on because it was always raining. It was pretty muddy. A few minutes later, the girls from Camp Botshagotta arrived.

"You're going to *lose*, Arlo!" Andrea shouted as she walked past us.

"Your *face* is gonna lose!" I shouted back at her.

We glared at the girls across the field, and they glared back at us. It was a lot like last night's social.

"Welcome to Color War Day!" Uncle Ahdoanwanna hollered into a bullhorn.

"It will be the best of seven games, like the World Series. The first camp to win four will be the winner. Game One will be Tug-of-War."

In the middle of the field was a long, thick rope. The Ahdoanwanna boys lined up on one side of the rope and the Botshagotta girls lined up on the other side.

In a tug-of-war, each team pulls on

the rope and tries to pull the other team toward them. We all picked up the rope.

"This is gonna be a piece of cake," Ryan said to me.

Huh? What did cake have to do with anything? Why was everybody always talking about cake?

"On your mark! Get set!" shouted Uncle Ahdoanwanna. "Pull!"

We pulled. I thought it would be easy,

but the girls pulled back hard. We pulled back harder. So did they. The rope wasn't moving one way or the other. It was hard to hold on. The girls were *strong*.

"It's slipping!" Neil shouted.

The rope was pulling me forward. It was hard to hold on.

Finally, the girls pulled us over the line. Everybody was falling all over everybody else. We had mud all over us. It was gross.

"Camp Botshagotta wins Game One!" shouted Uncle Ahdoanwanna. The girls went crazy, yelling and screaming their heads off.

"GIRLS RULE! BOYS DROOL!" they chanted.

Okay, so they won Game 1. That only made us more determined to beat them. Game 2 was Hula-Hooping. The counselors passed out twenty Hula-Hoops randomly, ten to the girls and ten to the boys. Whichever team had the last hula hooper who was still hula-hooping would be the winner.

"Oh, we got this!" shouted one of the girls from Camp Botshagotta.

The only boy in my bunk to get a

Hula-Hoop was Candyman, so all we could do was cheer him on.

"On your mark! Get set!" shouted Uncle Ahdoanwanna. "Hula!"

All twenty kids started hula-hooping. A few of them didn't know how to do it, and their hoops dropped to the ground right away. But most of the kids were pretty good.

One by one, the hoops dropped to the ground. Finally, it was down to two kids, Candyman and a girl from Camp Botshagotta. They must have hula-hooped for ten minutes. You could tell they were both really tired.

And then, the girl looked like she was going to pass out. She dropped her hoop.

"Camp Ahdoanwanna wins Game Two!" shouted Uncle Ahdoanwanna.

"Go, Candyman!" I shouted. We all high-fived Candyman. He told us he is training to be a professional hula hooper when he grows up. That guy is weird.

Now it was tied at one game each.

The Color War went on all day, except for a break for lunch. We won Game 3, which was Capture the Flag. Camp Botshagotta won Game 4—Squirt Blaster Battle. They also won Game 5—Relay Races. But we won Game 6—the Smelliest Shoe Contest.

It was all tied up again. Camp Ahdoanwanna had won three games, and Camp

Botshagotta had won three games.

"This is it," announced Uncle Ahdoan-wanna. "Game Seven is for all the marbles!"

Huh? What do marbles have to do with anything?

"Game Seven is the Bed Race," hollered Uncle Ahdoanwanna. "Each camp has to pick up a bed with one camper on it and carry it fifty yards. One bunk from each side will represent their camp. For Camp Botshagotta, it will be the Flowers. For Camp Ahdoanwanna, it will be the Owls."

"HOOT, HOOT, HOOT!" we chanted. "WE DON'T GIVE A HOOT!"

"We are definitely going to *crush* them this time!" said Michael.

Some counselors carried two beds out to the middle of the field. They set up a finish line fifty yards away. The Owls ran over to one bed, and a bunk of girls from Camp Botshagotta ran over to the other one. Neil is the lightest guy in our bunk, so we decided he should ride our bed.

"On your mark! Get set!" shouted Uncle Ahdoanwanna. "Oh, one more thing. Before you race, you have to *make* your bed."

WHAT?! I don't know how to make a bed.

"Do you know how to make a bed?" I whispered to Ryan.

"I've never made a bed in my life," he replied.

"Me neither," said Neil and Candyman.

"My mom always tells me to make my bed," said Michael. "But I never did it."

The counselors brought over a bunch of sheets, pillows, pillowcases, and blankets.

"On your mark! Get set! Go!" shouted Uncle Ahdoanwanna. "Make your bed!"

We ran around our bed, grabbing at the sheet and trying to put it over the mattress, but the corners kept slipping off. While we were doing that, Ryan struggled to put the pillowcases on the pillows. Neil tried to put the blanket on the bed, but we weren't finished putting on the sheet yet.

I looked over at the girls. They made their bed in about five seconds. One of them hopped on top, and the others picked up their bed.

"Hurry up!" I shouted at the guys.

The girls were halfway to the finish line when we finally got our bed made. It was pretty messy, but it was made. Neil hopped on, and the rest of us picked up the bed.

"Go! Go! Go!" Neil shouted.

We went as fast as we could, but the bed was really heavy and the girls had a big head start. It looked like we were catching up, but they crossed the finish line a few feet ahead of us.

"Camp Botshagotta wins Game Seven, and the Color War!" shouted Uncle Ahdoanwanna.

The girls were jumping all over each other. Me and the guys were out of breath and panting.*

The evening activity was a scavenger hunt, but none of us could get into it. We were upset about losing the Color War.

"I can't believe Camp Botshagotta beat us," Michael whispered after Uncle Ray flipped off the light for the night and left.

"We need to get revenge," Candyman whispered.

---

*That means we were wearing pants.

"But how?" whispered Ryan.

"We could sneak over to Camp Botshagotta," I whispered, "and steal the underwear off their clothesline."

"Let's *do* it!" said Neil.

"And we should put the underwear up on our flagpole!" I suggested.

We all got out of bed, put on our sneakers, grabbed flashlights, and tiptoed to the door of the bunk. No counselors were around. The coast was clear.

We sneaked outside. The path behind our bunk led to the lake. And on the other side of the lake was Camp Botshagotta. We were sneaking around the trees like secret agents. It was cool.

"This is gonna be great!" whispered Ryan.

And you'll never believe what happened next. Uncle Ahdoanwanna jumped out from behind a tree!

"Where do you boys think you're going?" he demanded.

I looked at Ryan. Ryan looked at Michael. Michael looked at Neil. Neil looked at Candyman. Candyman looked at me. We were all looking at each other.

"We have a dentist appointment," I said.

"Go back to your bunk," said Uncle Ahdoanwanna.

Bummer in the summer!

The End of Everything

11

"RISE AND SHINE!" announced Uncle Ahdoanwanna the next morning.

It was Friday, the last day of camp. We got dressed and went outside to pledge the allegiance. That's when the weirdest thing in the history of the world happened.

We gathered in a big circle around the flagpole for assembly. Well, that's not the weird part because we do that every morning. The weird part was when we looked up at the flagpole. You'll never believe in a million hundred years what was up there.

I'm not gonna tell you.

Okay, okay, I'll tell you.

IT WAS MY UNDERWEAR!

"Somebody snuck into our bunk and stole my underwear!" I shouted. "It had to be Andrea!"

"Ooooh," said Ryan. "Andrea stole A.J.'s underwear and hung it from the flagpole! They must be in *love*!"

"When are you gonna get married?" asked Michael.

After they took down my underwear and put up the flag, it started raining. Of course! So instead of pickleball, we had to go to arts and farts, where we made lanyards with Aunt Nancy. Do you know what a lanyard is? It's this plastic thing you wear around your neck so you can hang stuff from it.*

The whole week, we never played pickleball. We never went rock climbing. We never had archery. But we had plenty of mosquitoes, bees, ants, flies, mice, and spiders. One of the bunks had a *bat* fly into it. That must have been interesting.

The most exciting part of the week was when the porta-potty man came with this cool truck to empty out the porta-potties.

---

*Why would I want to hang something from my neck?

Now *that's* a tough job. When he was done, we all stood up and gave him a standing ovation.

Finally, it was the last night of camp. We went out to the woods, and all the campers gathered in a big circle. The counselors made a bonfire in the middle, and we toasted marshmallows. Yum!

Some guy came out with a guitar. He said his name was Uncle Howie, but we were supposed to call him "The Maestro."

"Hey, campers!" he shouted. "Are you boys up for a sing-along?"

"No!"

"Here's a little song I made up," he said. "You sing it to the tune of 'Over There.'"

And then he started singing . . .

Underwear! Underwear!
Send a pair, send a pair, I can wear!
For I left mine lying, on the line drying,
I need them now but they're not there . . .

That song was pretty cool, but after Andrea stole my underwear and put it up on the flagpole, I wasn't really in the mood to sing that song.

After that, we all had to sing "This Land Is Your Land," "Ain't No Flies on Us," "I Like Bananas," "Do Your Ears Hang Low," "Home on the Range," "Little Bunny Foo Foo," "On Top of Spaghetti," "B-I-N-G-O," "I'm Being Swallowed by a Boa

Constrictor," "The Ants Go Marching," "If You're Happy and You Know It," "The Wheels on the Bus," and a million hundred other boring songs.

When the fire died down and all the marshmallows were gone, the counselors said we could go out in the field and look at the stars before going back to our bunks. We got down on the grass and looked up at the sky.

"WOW," I said, which is "MOM" upside down. I had never seen so many stars at once.

"This is awesome," Ryan said. "There are probably a billion of them up there."

"A bazillion," I said. "Maybe we'll see a shooting star."

"Where do you think it ends?" asked Neil.

"Where does *what* end?" asked Michael.

"The universe," Neil replied. "It seems like it must go on forever."

"But it has to end *some*where," said Ryan.

Candyman had been pretty quiet as we gazed up at the sky.

"The sun is just another star," he told us. "In five billion years, it will run out of hydrogen and become a red giant hot enough to boil the oceans. The gravitational forces will pull all the gases to the center, and the sun will engulf Mercury, Venus, and Earth."

It was quiet for a minute or two.

"Wait," I said. *"What?"*

"The sun is gonna fade out in a giant spinning cloud of gas and dust," said Candyman. "Then the universe will collapse into itself and the planet we call Earth will disintegrate."

It was quiet for a minute or two. And then . . .

Everybody jumped up and started running around, yelling and screaming and hooting and hollering and freaking out.

"Help!" shouted Michael. "The sun is going to explode!"

"Run for your lives!" shouted Neil.

"The world is gonna end!" Ryan shouted.

"WE'RE ALL GOING TO DIE!" I shouted.

* * *

In the morning, we had to pack up our stuff and get ready to go home. After breakfast, a convoy of minivans started rolling into the parking lot. Parents were arriving to pick up their kids.

Everybody was crying and hugging each other. I didn't want anybody to see me cry, but everybody else was crying so I guess it was okay for me to cry too. I hugged Aunt Kim, Uncle Ray, Aunt Nancy, Uncle Howie, and everybody else. I even hugged Candyman when he left.

Most of the kids were gone by the time my mom and dad finally showed up. When they got out of the car, I ran over and gave them a big hug.

"We're sorry," my dad said. "We just got

your letter. We didn't know you were having such a terrible time."

"Your father and I had such fond memories of summer camp," my mom said. "We thought it would be the same for you."

They put my duffel bag into the trunk, and I climbed into the back seat.

"Say goodbye," my dad said as we pulled out of the parking lot. "I guess you'll never see this place again."

I thought about everything that happened in the last week. I almost drowned. I had to kiss a dead moose. I had to slow dance with Andrea. I had a million hundred mosquito bites. I drank a glass full of ketchup, mustard, and other gross stuff. I

got poison ivy. A skunk ran in our bunk.
We lost the bed race.

"Uh . . . " I said.

"Did you forget something, A.J.?" asked
my mom.

"No," I replied, wiping the tears from my eyes. "Can I go back next summer?"

Well, that's pretty much what happened at Camp Ahdoanwanna. Maybe my parents will let me come back next summer. Maybe smooching will be made illegal. Maybe they'll put toilets into cars. Maybe Candyman will tunnel out of camp with a spoon. Maybe a ghost will eat all the left-handed kids. Maybe I'll get to play laser tag and pickleball. Maybe penguins will slow dance. Maybe everybody will stop talking about cake. Maybe we'll find a way to stop the universe from collapsing.

But it won't be easy!

There's a Skunk in My Bunk!

WEIRD EXTRAS!

★ Summer Camp Facts

★ Summer Camp Word Search

★ Summer Camp Crossword

SUMMER CAMP FACTS

Hi there, campers! This is Professor A.J. I have a PhD in awesomeness. Since this is the My Weird School summer camp special, I thought I would tell you about the history of summer camps. I'm a professor, which means I know everything.

Summer camps first started back in 1943 by this guy named Bob Camp. He had a really sunny personality, so everybody called him "Summer." Yeah, that was his name, Bob Summer Camp.

Wait a minute, Arlo!

Oh no! Here comes the Human Homework Machine.

Arlo, you know perfectly well that there's no such person as Bob Summer Camp. You made that up.

So what? Kids won't know the difference. They're not going to check the facts on this.

But I will! The truth is, the first summer camp was started in 1861, in Connecticut. It was called the Gunnery Camp, and the owners were Frederick and Abigail Gunn. They saw it as a way for kids to escape the city during the hot summer and connect with nature.

Lots more summer camps opened in the 1870s and 1880s, mostly in New England, and just for boys. Camps for girls started up in the 1890s. These days, kids can go to all different kinds of summer camps. There are camps for the arts, magic, computers, math, sports, performing arts, and even cooking. There are more than fifteen *thousand* summer camps in the United States, and about twenty-six *million* campers.

Thank you, Miss Know-It-All. But as I was saying, Bob Summer Camp—

Quiet, Arlo!

FUN GAMES AND WEIRD WORD PUZZLES

SUMMER CAMP WORD SEARCH

Directions: Twelve words are hidden in this jumble of letters. Can you find them all?

```
C U A I N F I R M A R Y H B V
O D V I S E V I A B X U M K C
U J R O T F L A S H L I G H T
N J F W L U H W O T G Y V I F
S G J W C L U M D G F S C L W
E K X Y L W E V F R L E A Z N
L R A L Z S Y Y E M I X N B E
O B L X I Q T P B Q P F T D E
R C A C N M E K T A F U E V R
K Z K N U B N S Z D L M E D C
Y Q E O P S R P L G O L N C S
O D O N R Y O H Q K P N J A N
C N P G N I M M I W S I H C U
E B O L Q M O S Q U I T O E S
A F M P Z S J H T L X I A G B
```

COUNSELOR   BUNK
SWIMMING   LAKE
INFIRMARY
HOMESICK   CANTEEN
VOLLEYBALL   MOSQUITOES
FLASHLIGHT   FLIPFLOPS
SUNSCREEN

SUMMER CAMP CROSSWORD

Directions: Use the clues below to fill in this crossword puzzle. (Hint: All the answers have something to do with summer camp.)

Across:

1. You need 'em to make s'mores
2. A walk in the woods
3. Rub two sticks together
4. Quite a racket
5. You make them at camp

Down:

6. Target sport
7. You pitch them
8. Fun game, sort of like dodgeball
9. You sleep in them
10. Itsy-bitsy climber

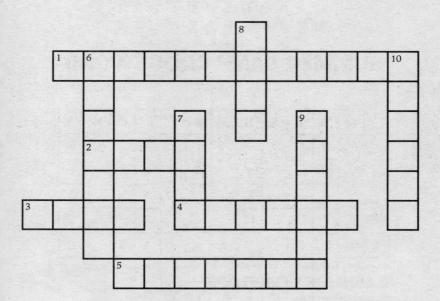

ANSWER KEY

SUMMER CAMP WORD SEARCH

```
C U A I N F I R M A R Y H B V
C O D V I S E V I A B X U M K C
O U J R O T F L A S H L I G H T
U N J F W L U H W O T G Y V I F
N S G J W C L U M D G F S C L W
S E K X Y L W E V F R L E A N Z
E L R A L Z S Y Y E M I X N B E
L O B L X I Q T P B Q P F T E D
O R C A C N M E K T A F U E R C
R K Z K N U B N S Z D L M E N S
Y Q E O P S R P L G O L N C N U
O D O N R Y O H Q K P N J A S U
C N P G N I M M I W S I H C U
E B O L Q M O S Q U I T O E S
A F M P Z S J H T L X I A G B
```

SUMMER CAMP CROSSWORD

Across:
1. MARSHMALLOWS
2. HIKE
3. FIRE
4. TENNIS
5. FRIENDS

Down:
6. ARCHERY
7. TENT
8. GALA
9. CABIN
10. SPIDER